For Malcolm
J.D.
For my little brother James
R.C.

First published 2012 by Macmillan Children's Books
This edition published 2014 by Macmillan Children's Books
a division of Macmillan Publishers Limited
20 New Wharf Road, London N1 9RR
Basingstoke and Oxford
Associated companies throughout the world
www.panmacmillan.com

ISBN: 978-1-4472-6792-8

1 3 5 7 9 8 6 4 2

A CIP catalogue record for this book is available from the British Library.

Printed in China

Julia Donaldson

THE PAPER DOLLS

WORLD RECORD SPECIAL EDITION

Illustrated by
Rebecca Cobb

MACMILLAN CHILDREN'S BOOKS

There was once a girl who
had tiger slippers

and a ceiling with
stars on it

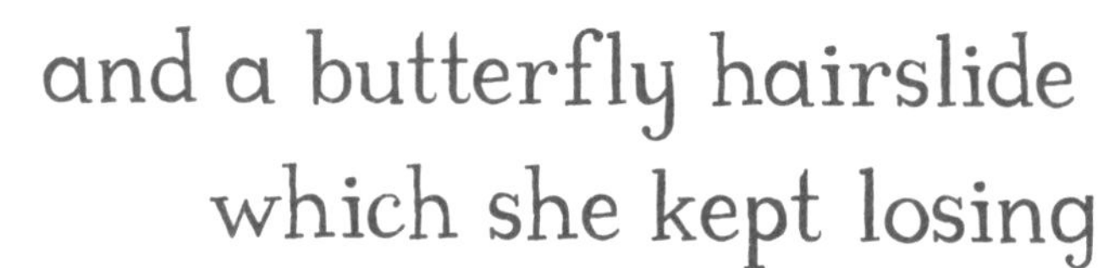

and a butterfly hairslide
which she kept losing

and two goldfish

and a nice mother who helped
her to make some paper dolls.

They were Ticky and Tacky
and Jackie the Backie
and Jim with two noses
and Jo with the bow.

And they danced

and they jumped

and they sang.

And they met a dinosaur
who clawed and roared,
and said, "I'm going to get you!"

But the paper dolls sang,

"You can't get us. Oh no no no!
We're holding hands and we won't let go.
We're Ticky and Tacky and Jackie the Backie
And Jim with two noses and Jo with the bow!"

And they jumped . . .

. . . on to a bus

and rode to a farmyard,
and danced with the pigs.

Then they lay on a rooftop and stared at the stars,
till a tiger slunk out of his den
and he crouched and snarled
and said, "I'll leap up and catch you!"

But the paper dolls sang,

“You can’t catch us. Oh no no no!
We’re holding hands and we won’t let go.

We're Ticky and Tacky and Jackie the Backie
And Jim with two noses and Jo with the bow!"

And they floated . . .

. . . down the stairs

and they danced round
the honey pot

and kicked crumbs
and explored an island

till a fierce crocodile grinned his grin
and gnashed his teeth
and said, "I'm coming to crunch you!"

But the paper dolls laughed, and sang,

"You can't crunch us. Oh no no no!
We're holding hands and we won't let go.

We're Ticky and Tacky and Jackie the Backie
And Jim with two noses and Jo with the bow!"

And they hopped . . .

. . . into the garden

and they sniffed the flowers
and chatted to a ladybird

and lay down in a
forest of grass.

But along came a boy
with a pair of scissors
and he said, "I'll SNIP you!"

And he did.
He snipped them into tiny little pieces
and he said, “You’re gone for ever.”

But the paper dolls sang,

"We're not gone. Oh no no no!
We're holding hands and we won't let go.
We're Ticky and Tacky and Jackie the Backie
And Jim with two noses and Jo with the bow!"

And the pieces all joined together,

and the paper dolls flew . . .

. . . into the little girl's memory
where they found white mice and fireworks,
and a starfish soap,
and a kind granny,
and the butterfly hairslide,
and more and more lovely things each day
and each year.

And the girl grew . . .

. . . into a mother

who helped her own little girl
make some paper dolls.

They were Poppy and Pinkie
and Binky the Blinkie,
and Fred with one eyebrow,
and Flo with the bow.

And they jumped,

and they danced,

and they sang.

The record was broken on the 11th November 2013 at the Royal Festival Hall in London. Thousands of people from all over the world sent in dolls, from places as far away as South Korea, Argentina and New Zealand. It took almost nine hours to lay out all the dolls and stick them together, and Julia Donaldson and Rebecca Cobb helped complete the chain.

Rebecca Cobb drew herself with Julia Donaldson.

The chain measured 4.54km in length, which is nearly two kilometres longer than the previous record! 4.54km is almost three miles, and is equivalent to 40 football pitches, 61 jumbo jets, or 80,000 jelly babies laid end to end. We donated 10p per doll to Save the Children, raising over £4,500.

How to make your very own paper dolls.

Trace these dolls onto a sheet of paper.

Fold up the paper, following the dotted lines.

Carefully cut out your dolls using the top outline as a guide.

Now get creative and decorate your dolls! Here are some ideas: